To the lovely couples who feed us: Jeff & Suzanne,
John & Shannon, Pat & Maiya, Ben & Tammy—M. S.

To my mom, who was (and is) wise enough
to let me be mild with a little wild—B. L.

SIMON & SCHUSTER BOOKS FOR YOUNG READERS • An imprint of Simon & Schuster Children's Publishing Division • 1230 Avenue of the Americas, New York, New York 10020
Text copyright © 2009 by Maurice Send-up • Illustrations copyright © 2009 by Bonnie Leick • All rights reserved, including the right of reproduction in whole or in part in any form. • SIMON &
SCHUSTER BOOKS FOR YOUNG READERS is a trademark of Simon & Schuster, Inc. • For information about special discounts for bulk purchases, please contact Simon & Schuster Special Sales
at 1-866-506-1949 or business@simonandschuster.com. • The Simon & Schuster Speakers Bureau can bring authors to your live event. For more information or to book an event, contact
the Simon & Schuster Speakers Bureau at 1-866-248-3049 or visit our website at www.simonspeakers.com. • The text for this book is set in Candara. • The illustrations for this book are
rendered in watercolor with the linework being done in graphite mechanical .3-mm pencil on Strathmore 500 Series Bristol 4-ply vellum. • Manufactured in the United States of America
10 9 8 7 6 5 4 3 2 1 • CIP data for this book is available from the Library of Congress. • ISBN 978-1-4169-9551-7

first edition

WHERE THE mild THINGS ARE

a very meek parody

By
Maurice Send-up

Illustrated by
Bonnie Leick

Simon & Schuster Books for Young Readers
NEW YORK LONDON TORONTO SYDNEY

There was a wonderful land filled

with horrible monsters.

They had appalling horns and appalling claws and appalling fur and were drawn with far too many lines, which made them very special.

But Mog wasn't horrible at all. He'd sit quietly in his room, reading the dullest books ever written.

Every couple of days his mother would check to make sure that he wasn't dead.

One day Mog's parents caught him gently petting a kitten. "Stop playing with your food!" growled Mog's father.

His parents sent him to bed without any dinner. This made Mog very unhappy.

(But it made the kitten very happy indeed.)

Mog sat in bed.

And slowly his bed turned into a car.
A very monstrous car.
A 1974 AMC Gremlin.

So Mog drove off
in search of adventure.
But he drove very slowly
and only visited the
most boring places.

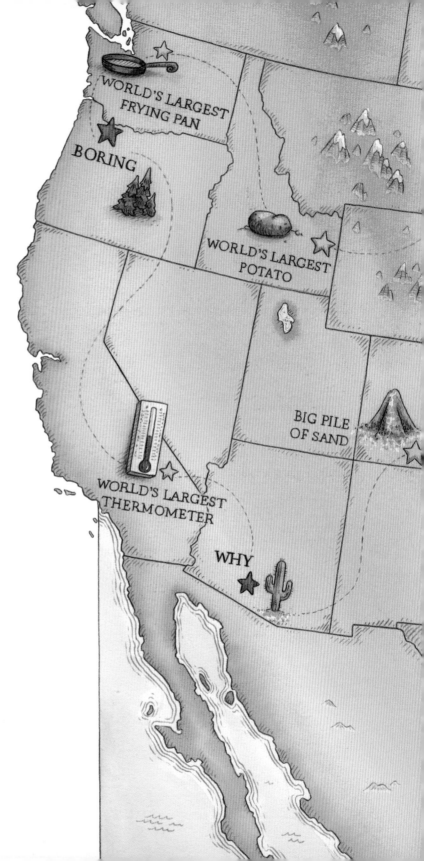

WORLD'S LARGEST
FRYING PAN

BORING

WORLD'S LARGEST
POTATO

BIG PILE
OF SAND

WORLD'S LARGEST
THERMOMETER

WHY

Finally, Mog found the perfect spot: Dullsville. And there he
met some very mild creatures. A Homemaker whose house was
much cleaner than yours will ever be.

A Comedian who wasn't all that funny. A very, very, very, very, very rich Nerd. And a boring man who had been Vice President, and had almost become President but not quite.

The mild creatures made Mog the President of Dullsville.
The very boring man was elected Vice President.
Again.

Mog gave a very long speech that put everyone to sleep.
Including himself.
After that, they had lots of adventures.

One day the mild creatures replaced their regular
lightbulbs with energy-saving lightbulbs.

Then they replaced their energy-saving lightbulbs with slow-burning safety candles.

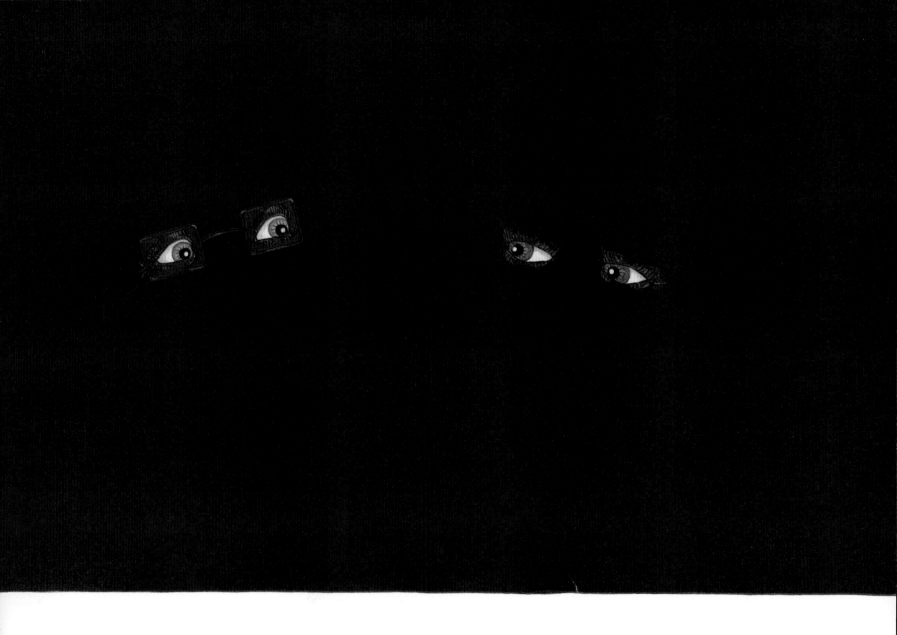

When the candles went out,

they sat in the dark.

Mog was so bored, he let out a mighty roar.
He stamped his appalling feet
and gnashed his appalling teeth.
Then he jumped into his AMC Gremlin
and drove away as fast as he could.

"He's wasting gas by driving that fast,"
said the Vice President.

When Mog got home, he ran to his parents,
wrapped his arms around them,
and kicked them both in the shins
for putting him through all this.

His parents were overjoyed at what
an appalling monster he'd become.

(The kitten was not so happy.)